This Little Tiger Book Belongs To:

_____

_____

_____

LITTLE TIGER PRESS
An imprint of Magi Publications
1 The Coda Centre, 189 Munster Road, London SW6 6AW
www.littletigerpress.com
This paperback edition published in 2002
First published in Great Britain 2002
2002 © Diane and Christyan Fox

ISBN 1 85430 770 3
1 3 5 7 9 10 8 6 4 2

Spaceman PiggyWiggy

Christyan and Diane Fox

LITTLE TIGER PRESS

Whenever I lie in bed at night, I look at the stars above, and dream of what it would be like to be a daring spaceman!

I would climb into my rocket dressed in my special spacesuit and prepare for lift-off.

I would need lots of training to learn how to use all the controls. Then . . .

Blast off into outer space!

In space everything floats . . .

so it would be
very difficult to
eat and drink!

I would have to go outside the spaceship....

for a space walk.

We would land on
exciting, faraway
planets...

and make
new friends.

But I hope
there would
be time to
do all these
things ...

and be back in time for breakfast.

I spy a book from Little Tiger Press

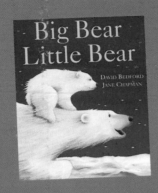

For information regarding any of the above titles or for our catalogue, please contact us:
Little Tiger Press, 1 The Coda Centre, 189 Munster Road, London SW6 6AW, UK
Telephone: 020 7385 6333 Fax: 020 7385 7333
e-mail: info@littletiger.co.uk
www.littletigerpress.com